SLIDES INTO SUMMER

created by

JAY ALBEE

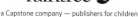

a Capstone company — publishers for children

Raintree is an imprint of Capstone Global Library Limited, a company
incorporated in England and Wales having its registered office at 264
Banbury Road, Oxford, OX2 7DY - Registered company number: 6695582

www.raintree.co.uk
myorders@raintree.co.uk

Designed by Nathan Gassman

Special thanks to Manu Shadow Velasco for their consultation.

978 1 3982 5512 8

British Library Cataloguing in Publication Data
A full catalogue record for this book is available from the British Library.

Printed and bound in India.

CONTENTS

CHAPTER ONE
THE THIRD OF JULY 8

CHAPTER TWO
MISSION FOR MORE COCONUT 18

CHAPTER THREE
AMBROSIA AND EMPANADAS 30

CHAPTER FOUR
THE FOURTH OF JULY 40

CHAPTER FIVE
SUMMER SOFTBALL
(AND KICKBALL TOO). 48

CHAPTER SIX
NOTHING SAYS CELEBRATION
LIKE FIREWORKS 56

I'M RILEY!

I LOVE SO MANY THINGS! I LOVE CRAFTING.

THE ONLY THING BETTER THAN MAKING A MESS IS MAKING COOL STUFF.

I LOVE MY PARENTS, MY COUSINS AND MY FRIENDS.

I LOVE DOGS AND CATS . . .

AND BIRDS AND FISH . . .

AND DRAGONS AND UNICORNS AND ALL ANIMALS!

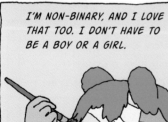

I'M NON-BINARY, AND I LOVE THAT TOO. I DON'T HAVE TO BE A BOY OR A GIRL.

I CAN JUST BE ME!

MX AUDE TEACHES HELPFUL TERMS

Cisgender: Cisgender (or cis) people identify with the gender written on their birth certificate. They are usually boys or girls.

Gender identity: Regardless of the gender on a person's birth certificate, they decide their gender identity. It might change over time. A person's interests, clothes and behaviour might be traditionally associated with their gender identity, or they might not.

Honorific: Young people use honorifics when they talk to or about adults, especially teachers. Mr is the honorific for a man, Mrs or Ms for a woman and Mx is the gender-neutral honorific often used for non-binary people. It is pronounced "mix". Non-binary people may also use Mr, Mrs or Ms.

LGBTQ+: This stands for lesbian, gay, bisexual (also pansexual), transgender, queer. There are lots of ways people describe their gender and attraction. These are just a few of those ways. The + sign means that there are many, many more, and they are all included in the acronym LGBTQ+.

Non-binary: Non-binary people have a gender identity other than boy or girl. They may be neither, both, a combination or sometimes one and sometimes the other.

Pronouns: Pronouns are how people refer to themselves and others (she/her, they/them, he/him, etc.). Pronouns often line up with gender identity (especially for cis people), but not always. It's best to ask a person what pronouns they like to use.

Queer: An umbrella term for people who identify as LGBTQ+.

Transgender: Transgender (or trans) people do not identify with the gender listed on their birth certificate. They might identify as the other binary gender, both genders or another gender identity.

CHAPTER ONE

THE THIRD OF JULY

"Why is it called softball?" asked
Trudy. "The ball isn't actually soft, is it?"

Trudy was one of Riley's younger
cousins. She was visiting.

"Maybe it gets soft when it rains?"
suggested Riley.

"Or when someone hits a home run?" added Trudy.

"How would that work?" asked Marisol.

Marisol was one of Riley's older cousins and Trudy's big sister. Trudy was seven and Marisol was thirteen. Riley was in between them.

It was the same story with the rest of the extended family. Riley had plenty of younger cousins. They had plenty of older cousins too. Riley thought Marisol was the coolest. But Riley did not have any cousins their own age.

Marisol shook her head. "It's called softball because the ball used to be soft. Like, way back when the game first started. It used to be played inside."

"Ah," said Riley knowingly, "to keep the ball out of the rain."

Marisol rolled her eyes, but she was smiling. She smacked the softball into her glove. She was practising a finger hold that would make the ball curve. She'd only been playing softball for a year, but she loved it.

Every year on the Fourth of July weekend, Mama's extended family had a family reunion and a softball game. This year was the 25th reunion.

Trudy, Marisol and their parents were in town for the party. Trudy and Marisol were staying with the Reynoldses, while their mum and stepdad stayed with Abuelita.

When Riley was little, they called Marisol and Trudy their "summer cousins" because that's the only time they saw them. The name stuck for the whole family.

No one could remember why the annual family reunion included a softball game. But Mum remembered that when she was a teenager, they added a kickball game for the younger kids too.

Riley and their dad were screen printing the Summer Softball T-shirts. Riley's dad loved making matching T-shirts for everyone, and everyone loved wearing them.

"Did you know that softball was invented in Chicago?" Riley's dad asked.

Trudy's eyes went wide. "Really? That's where I live!"

Dad laughed. "And do you know what it was called before they settled on softball?"

Trudy's eyes went even wider. She shook her head slowly.

"Mushball," said Dad.

Trudy squeal-laughed. "Mushball!"

"That's way better than softball!" Riley laughed.

Standing at an easel in the middle of Dad's home art studio, Riley dipped an old toothbrush into a dish of red fabric paint. With their thumb, Riley flicked the paint onto a printed T-shirt. They stepped back, tilted their head and nodded.

"This one's ready," Riley said.

Marisol put down her ball and glove. She carefully carried the T-shirt from Riley's easel to the drying rack, where slim wire shelves kept the shirts separate. Screen printing could get very messy very quickly. It was important to have someone with clean hands to assist.

Last year, Riley had been the clean-handed assistant. But it turned out to be impossible for Riley to be around paint and not use it! Clean hands? Not so much. Every single shirt had a smudge.

This year, Riley had helped Dad with the design. Since it was the 25th anniversary reunion, Dad wanted the design to be extra special. With Riley, he had sketched out lots of ideas. But it was Riley's brainwave to add uniquely splattered fireworks to each shirt. Nothing said celebration more than fireworks!

Riley had been practising the paint-splatter-firework technique in their sketchbook all week. They ran their thumb across a paint-dipped toothbrush on page after page after page.

Today, the first couple of T-shirts were a bit wonky, but the splatters were getting better each time. They were starting to really look like explosions of light launched into the sky.

"I'm ready too, Mari," said Dad.

Marisol carried fresh T-shirts to Dad's screen-printing station. She carried printed T-shirts to Riley's firework station. And finally, she carried the finished T-shirts to the drying rack. They'd been at it all afternoon!

"Last one!" said Marisol, smoothing the last T-shirt under Dad's raised screen.

Then squeeze and splatter and rack and they were done! High fives all round!

"Time to clean up!" said Dad.

Riley and Dad washed their hands and rinsed the screens and toothbrushes. Marisol and Trudy wiped some stray splatters off the easel. All four of them gathered and folded the dust sheet from underneath it.

"Looks good," said Dad. He checked the time on his phone. "I have to take some things over to your Abuelita's for tomorrow. And don't forget, Ry, you said you'd help your mum."

"Oh, right," said Riley.

They had forgotten. Getting ready for the tournament seemed to get busier and busier each year. Or maybe it was always this busy and Riley was old enough to finally notice.

CHAPTER TWO

A MISSION FOR MORE COCONUT

Riley, Trudy and Marisol trotted into the kitchen. Riley's mum was preparing food. She was also singing and dancing to a playlist of her favourite songs.

"Hi, Mum. Can we help?" Riley asked.

Mum grinned and flicked her hips. She grabbed Riley's hand and spun them round. Riley took Trudy's hand and Mum grabbed Marisol's. Mum danced them all around the kitchen table. The song ended with a powerful, sustained high note. Everyone clutched their hearts and belted out the final wail.

"We won't win any talent shows." Mum laughed. "That's for sure."

"No kidding," Marisol heartily agreed. She peered into a giant mixing bowl. "What are you making?"

"That," said Mum, "is ambrosia salad."

She scooped her wooden spoon into the mixing bowl and brought out a fluffy, white, chunky mixture. She let it drop off the spoon. It fell back into the bowl with a *plop* and a *splat*.

"What is it?" asked Trudy.

Riley's eyes went wide. "Haven't you had it before? We always make it for the big summer reunion!"

Mum laughed. "Just one of the dozens of traditions we've picked up over the twenty-five years."

Riley said, "It's whipped cream and yogurt and tinned fruit cocktail and fresh clementine slices and coconut and marshmallows and those bright red, glazed, kind of see-through cherries! Try it."

Marisol shook her head, but Trudy took a tiny bite.

"Oh, wow," she said. "That's . . . pretty weird."

"What?" said Riley. "It's the best!"

"Only you and your Abuelita think that, Ry," said Mum.

"And you too," said Riley, taking a bite. "Mmm!"

"Eh," said Mum. "Not really."

Riley frowned at Mum. They licked their lips. "I thought it was your favourite food?"

"It was when I was your age. But then one time I ate too much of it and made myself sick. Now I can't stand it," she said.

"What?!" squawked Riley.

"Don't tell Abuelita," said Mum. "It was a really big deal when she gave me the recipe and I started making it for the tournament. And I can handle making it for her. It makes her happy. But – tell me, what do you think of this batch?"

Riley took ambrosia salad very seriously. They took another bite, and then another one to make sure. "It's good. But it needs more coconut."

Mum took the spoon back. "Yeah, I ran out. I hoped it would be enough. Can you go to the bodega to get more?" Mum opened her purse and handed Riley some cash and then the empty coconut packet. "This kind."

"Okay," said Riley, taking the notes and the empty bag.

"You'll have to go to Ba Market. They won't have it at the corner shop. And get more glacé cherries if they have them. That's Abuelita's favourite part," Mum said.

"Okay," said Riley, heading for the door with Trudy and Marisol.

"And come straight back. I need you to fold the empanadas," Mum said.

"Okay," said Riley, opening the front door to the little terraced house.

"And get something for the three of you to share!" Mum continued.

"Okay, Mum!" Riley waited a second, holding the door handle. Did Mum have anything more to say? The only sound from the kitchen was an upbeat love song. "Okay, bye!"

"Are you still here?" Mum laughed. "Get going!"

Riley smiled and pulled the door closed

behind them.

YIP! YIP! YIP!

As soon as Riley and their cousins were on the pavement, they heard the barking. Sandy, the excited little terrier who lived across the street, saw them through her front window.

"Hi, Sandy!" Riley called out.

"*YIP! YIP! YIP!*" Trudy replied.

They all waved and headed up the street. They approached a neighbour sitting in the sun on her doorstep.

"Hi, Julia," said Riley. "We're going to the bodega. Do you need anything?"

"Ah," Julia sighed. "I was just thinking how nice an iced tea would be on a day like this." She pulled some cash out of her pocket and Riley took it. "You know the kind I like."

"Yes," said Riley.

Ba Market was two blocks away. It was the biggest bodega in the area. They sold all sorts of things that the smaller corner shops didn't, like shredded coconut! The owners, Mr and Mrs Chopra, always had warm smiles for everyone who came in. Today Mr Chopra was behind the counter. His turban was as blue as the summer sky.

"Oh!" Marisol said, breathing in deeply. "It smells amazing!"

She headed straight to the wall of spices at the back of the shop: bright yellow turmeric powder, greenish-brown seeds and a solid brick of something velvety-red. They all sat next to each other in plastic bags with labels. There were spiky cloves, star-shaped anise and sticks of cinnamon.

"Look at all this stuff!" Marisol beamed. She breathed in the warm, sweet scent and sighed. "I want to try them all!"

"It makes my nose tickle," said Trudy.

"I've got the coconut and the cherries," said Riley.

At the front of the shop, Riley took a can of iced tea from the drinks fridge and a packet of sour gummy sweets from the counter. Those were the cousins' favourite sweets.

"Thank you," said Riley when Mr

Chopra handed them their change.

"Have a good day," he replied with a big, big smile.

"Let's go!" Riley called to Marisol and Trudy.

On the walk back to Riley's, they all took turns taking a sweet. They closed their eyes, dipped their fingers into the packet and guessed what colour they would get. They didn't get a single guess right!

CHAPTER THREE

AMBROSIA AND EMPANADAS

Mum cut open the packets of coconut and glacé cherries. "Ry, you take over the ambrosia. Marisol and Trudy, come over to the table. I'll teach you how to fold empanadas."

She sat at the kitchen table with Trudy and Marisol. The table had a light dusting of flour on it. A packet of empanada pastry discs sat next to a big bowl of cooked onions, potato and green peppers, and a seasoned sausage called chorizo.

"What spices did you use?" asked Marisol, breathing deeply over the bowl.

"Cumin, smoked paprika, garlic powder and Mexican oregano," said Mum. "And lots of them!"

"I think I saw all those at Ba Market," said Marisol.

"I'm sure you did," said Mum. "They're used in all kinds of national cuisines. Ba Market is known for their spices. They are bestsellers! Now let's make some empanadas."

Mum took a circle of empanada pastry from the wrapped pile and put a spoonful of filling in the middle. Marisol and Trudy copied her. "Then fold the disc over, making sure the filling is nice and snug inside." They did. "Take a fork and press it around the edges to seal. Not too hard, but not too soft either."

"Like this?" asked Trudy.

The fork left neat little line imprints around the edge of the half-moon hand pie.

"Perfect," said Mum. "Now put the empanada on the baking paper and go again. Show me how it's done."

She watched as Marisol and Trudy each picked up another disc of pastry.

Meanwhile, standing on a step at the kitchen worktop, Riley added a bit of coconut to the ambrosia salad. They mixed it in and tasted it.

"This still doesn't taste right," Riley said, frowning.

They added another bit of coconut, mixed it in, and tasted. "Hmm, not yet."

They repeated this many times. How would they know if the mix was just right if they didn't keep tasting it? While they worked, they tried to whistle along to the song that was playing.

When the school year ended, Riley had decided that their summer project would be learning how to whistle. They imagined how much fun it would be to show their classmates after the break.

So far, they had discovered two things. Firstly, whistling was much harder than it looked. And secondly, there were different kinds of whistles. For example, Kwame, who ran the local craft shop, could whistle loudly and sharply with two fingers in his mouth. Mx Aude, the school librarian, could whistle loudly and sharply doing something weird with their top lip and teeth. Mr Russo, who lived across the street, could whistle a melody. He sounded like a bird.

As Riley mixed in more coconut, they puckered their lips and blew. Air came out, but not much sound. They sighed. They had thought there would be plenty of time to suss this thing out. But, so far, the summer had been even busier than the school year, which Riley didn't think was possible!

"You've got it," said Mum as Marisol and Trudy worked hard to finish their second empanadas. "Keep it up! I'll finish the pico de gallo."

She moved back to the worktop, where a bowl of chopped tomatoes and red onions was waiting. She glanced at the ambrosia salad. The bowl was not as full as it had been moments before.

"Riley! How much salad did you eat?" she asked.

"Not that much. It tastes just right now," said Riley, licking the mixing spoon.

"No more," said Mum, taking away the spoon and bowl. "You'll make yourself sick. And, I can tell you, ambrosia salad sick is the worst."

She covered the creamy fruit salad and put it in the fridge. "Go and fold empanadas before your insides turn to marshmallow."

Then she cut into a large bunch of coriander. A fresh citrusy smell filled the kitchen.

Riley sat at the kitchen table. Mum and Abuelita and all of Riley's aunts and uncles could do a fancy crimping fold to seal the pies. One day, Riley wanted to learn it too. But, for now, they would have to use a fork.

Marisol looked into the bowl. "This is going to take forever," she said.

"Not if we work together," Riley said.

They took a pastry disc and a spoonful of filling and plopped it down with attitude. And, with that, they all started working. They laughed and sang and folded what felt like a million empanadas.

Later, Marisol, Trudy and Riley had too much energy to sleep. Instead, they made up new rules for the card game Uno. They weren't sure who had won, but they all agreed that the new game was awesome.

CHAPTER FOUR

THE FOURTH OF JULY

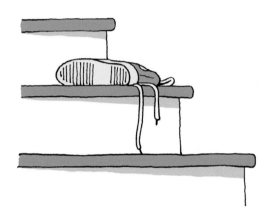

"Riley! Where is your other shoe?" Dad yelled from the living room.

He held one of Riley's shoes up in one hand. He pulled up sofa cushions in his search for the other.

"It's on my foot!" Riley yelled from their room. "Do you have the other one?"

"It's here! Come and put it on! Our lift will be here any minute!" Dad yelled back.

Mum, Trudy and Marisol were ready to go and were waiting.

Riley hurried into the living room. They walked lopsided with only one shoe on. Riley jammed their socked foot into their second shoe – and not a moment too soon!

Mum opened the front door of their little house. She waved to a minivan waiting in the narrow, one-way street. "That's Matty! Let's go!"

Matty was another of Riley's cousins. He lived near by. Riley's family didn't have a car, so Matty was giving them a lift to the softball ground.

"Hi, Matty! Thanks for picking us up,"
Mum said.

"You're welcome!" replied Matty.

Matty had just got his driving licence
and found any excuse to drive. Everyone
poured out of the Reynolds's house and
into Matty's parents' minivan. They took
with them a box of printed T-shirts, a big
tub of pico de gallo, two huge foil trays of
empanadas and the ambrosia salad.

Riley put on their seat belt and shifted
the cooler bag in their lap. Inside was
the ambrosia salad. It had been a busy
morning, but Riley had made checking on
the ambrosia a priority. They had made
extra-quadruple sure that it still tasted

right. It did. Every time. But they wished they had a spoon so they could check again. To make extra-quintuple sure.

When they arrived at the field, some of Mum's family were already there, laughing and talking. Some set up folding tables and gas canisters to keep food warm. Some were throwing a softball around. Others were playing tag.

"Riley! Look at you!" said Riley's oldest summer cousin, Oz. "Wow, you've grown. Last time I saw you, you were only this big." He placed his hand out about a foot lower than Riley.

Riley rolled their eyes. "Yeah, yeah. You're the fourth person to say that since we got here."

Oz laughed and hugged Riley. "You know, that was the first time I've ever said it. It felt weird! I used to hate it when people said it to me." He held a hand over his heart. "Never again, I promise!"

"T-shirts!" shouted Abuelita. "Where are the T-shirts?!" The family gathered around.

"Riley?" Dad asked. "Do you want to hand them out?"

"Yeah!" Riley beamed.

They folded back the top flaps of the box. The design was a well-kept secret each year. The reveal was a big deal!

For a second, Riley worried that nobody would know that the paint splatters were supposed to be fireworks.

Maybe they were too blobby.

Maybe Riley should have practised more.

Riley took a breath and held up a T-shirt. The family *oohed* and *aahed*. Abuelita gave Riley a big kiss on their cheek.

"Fireworks! You are very clever, Ry Ry."

Riley beamed even more.

Everyone slipped on their T-shirts, someone turned up the music and the party began.

CHAPTER FIVE

SUMMER SOFTBALL (AND KICKBALL TOO)

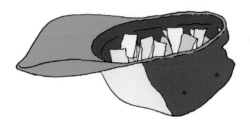

Trudy ran around the reunion from person to person, carrying paper, pen and her stepdad's peaked cap. Anyone who wanted to play softball put their name in the hat. The other game of the day was kickball.

"Riley? Mari? Abuelita?" Trudy asked.

"You bet," said Abuelita, taking a slip of paper and writing her name on it.

"Me too!" said Marisol, doing the same. It would be her first year playing softball at the reunion.

"Ha!" Trudy said, gloating. "You're scared that I'll beat you at kickball!"

Abuelita laughed at Trudy. "That's why I don't play kickball any more!" Abuelita squeezed Marisol tight. "Good for you. I hope we're on the same team." She turned to Riley. "What about you, Ry Ry?"

"Nah," said Riley. "I'm just getting the hang of kickball!"

"Yay!" Trudy hooted. She grinned wide at Riley.

Riley recognized that look. It was the same grin that Riley gave Marisol when they were Trudy's age. Riley realized that for Trudy, Riley was the coolest cousin! They felt light as a feather.

The softball players pulled names out of the hat, built teams and chose captains. At the same time, the kickball game kicked off. Riley was the oldest player this year. The oldest player always pitched.

"I'm not very good," said Riley, "but I'll do my best."

Riley couldn't pitch the ball very hard. But that was perfect for letting the little cousins kick it. The ball flew all over the field.

It flew furthest, though, when Riley got a chance to kick. Up, up and way into the outfield – where Trudy was waiting, arms outstretched. When she caught the ball, it knocked her over backwards, but she didn't let go!

Riley ran all the way into the outfield and hugged Trudy.

"Amazing catch!" they said.

Trudy beamed and brushed the grass off her bottom.

Then the game was over and the softball players took to the field. About half of the family was playing softball. The rest cheered, snacked and chatted.

The younger cousins made up a game. They took turns climbing onto a park bench and jumping off it. There really weren't any rules. Riley held the hands of the littlest cousin so he could jump safely too. After a while, Trudy led the younger cousins to the outfield. They sat in a circle and made daisy chains.

Riley bounced over to the equipment shed at the edge of the field. This is where the non-softball-playing older cousins were hanging out.

"Climb up, Ry!" called Matty from the flat roof of the squat concrete shed.

Riley climbed up the chain-link fence and hopped onto the roof. "Best view of the game!"

Riley sat down and the concrete felt warm on their legs.

"It's so cool that you can drive now," they said.

"Ha! It's wild. They gave me a licence! Me!" Matty laughed a fake-maniacal laugh. "Mum only lets me drive the van, though. Not exactly the coolest ride. But I've found a car, and I'm teaching myself to overhaul the engine. You see . . ."

Riley half listened while Matty went on and on about engines and transmissions and his grand plans for the car of his dreams.

Halfway through the game, the softball players paused for drinks and snacks. Riley came down from the shed roof, and the kids came in from the outfield. They festooned Riley and Marisol with daisy chains.

Then play started up again. Riley took an empanada in each hand and went to watch. Sitting together on the grass, Riley and Trudy laughed and cheered. One uncle ran to each base backwards. Another pitched with their eyes closed. Abuelita dived into second base. But they cheered the loudest when Marisol hit a home run.

NOTHING SAYS CELEBRATION LIKE FIREWORKS

At the end of the day, the sun had set and the youngest cousins were curled up in their parents' laps. The family gathered on folding chairs and picnic blankets to wait for the city fireworks.

Riley, tired and happy, sat by Abuelita. Mum, sitting next to them, held Riley's hand.

"Did you like the ambrosia salad this year, Abuelita?" asked Riley.

"I didn't have any, honey," she said.

"Well I can fix that!" Riley said.

They leaped off the chair and dashed over to the remains of the feast. Among the scraps of coleslaw, empanadas, pigs-in-blankets, hot dogs and Abuelita's mustardy potato salad, Riley found the ambrosia and two spoons.

"Look, Abuelita," Riley said. "There is just enough left for us to share. And – see – we put in extra glacé cherries just for you."

"Oh, honey," said Abuelita. "That's all yours. There's a reason I didn't have any yet. I don't like it!"

"What?" said Mum, sitting up suddenly. "I thought you did! I've been making it every year for you!"

Riley burst out laughing. So did Mum!

"I don't like it either!" she said.

Abuelita's laughter jiggled through her whole body, making Riley laugh harder. Abuelita wiped away a tear, but the giggles kept coming.

"Well, I like it enough for all of us!" Riley took a big bite.

Just then, the fireworks burst into the sky as bright as Riley's paint splatters. Riley leaned back in their chair. They *oohed* and *aahed* along with the whole family. Abuelita whistled at a particularly sparkly one.

Riley sat up sharply. "That's how I want to whistle! Can you teach me how to do it?"

Abuelita squeezed Riley's hand tight. "It's not an easy thing to explain, Ry. It took me a whole summer to learn when I was your age. Just keep trying and you'll get it, I promise."

Riley smiled and rubbed their tummy. They had eaten a little too much ambrosia salad . . . but not so much that they weren't already looking forward to eating it again next year.

THE END

DISCUSSION QUESTIONS

1. Some people have big families. Some people have small families. Family can include friends as well. Talk about your family.

2. Summertime often includes big gatherings. Do you like big social events or not? Talk about your answer.

3. Big parties often include lots of food. If you had to make some food for a party, what would you make and why?

WRITING PROMPTS

1. Riley looks up to Marisol. Trudy looks up to Riley. Write about a person you look up to.

2. This story focuses on the 4th July holiday called American Independence Day. It is celebrated by everyone in the United States. Write about your favourite holiday day.

3. If you could plan a friends and family reunion, what would it include? Write about the games and entertainment, when and where it would be and what kind of food you would eat.

MEET THE CREATORS

Jay Albee is the joint pen name for LGBTQ+ couple Jen Breach and J. Anthony. Between them, they've done lots of jobs: archaeologist, illustrator, ticket taker and bagel baker, but now they write and draw all day long in their house in Philadelphia, USA.

They have never had ambrosia salad, but they are sure it must be delicious.

Jen Breach

J. Anthony